D1145928

Piggo and the Nosebag

Pam Ayres

Illustrations by Andy Ellis

GUILD PUBLISHING

LONDON · NEW YORK · SYDNEY · TORONTO

This edition published 1990 by Guild Publishing,
by arrangement with BBC Books,
a division of BBC Enterprises Limited
First published 1990

Text © Pam Ayres 1990
Illustrations © Andy Ellis 1990
CN 6557

Set in Century Schoolbook by Goodfellow & Egan Ltd
Printed and bound in Great Britain by Cambus Litho Ltd, East Kilbride
Colour separations by Dot Gradations Ltd, Chelmsford
Jacket printed by Belmont Press Ltd, Northampton

Once in a fold of the hills, there was big house called Badgerwood.
Families came to visit it, and play, and have picnics in its beautiful park.
Behind the house was a Childrens Farmyard, with lots of animals. One of
the animals was a piglet, and his name was Piggo.

It was spring. There were chicks under the mother hen, a brown and white calf, two new lambs playing a game of balance-on-mum's-back, and a baby donkey with long grey ears. The cold days of winter had melted away and a bright sun shone warmly down.

Piggo was out for a walk. He was a round, pink, nosy little pig, with a curly tail. He stood on the bridge watching the black and yellow ducklings paddle furiously to keep up with their mother. He skipped over the wide smooth lawn to the fountain in the middle. Then, feeling suddenly very happy and full of beans as people sometimes do in the spring, he raced back across the garden to the farmyard where he lived.

As he skidded to a stop and looked brightly around he heard a terrible noise.

"Ooooooh . . ." groaned somebody sadly. "Oooooooh, dear me . . . I don't know, I'm sure . . . Ooooooh dear."

Piggo was horrified! Who could be feeling so sad on such a lovely day? He looked around.

The sad voice groaned on. It was coming from behind Piggo, from inside the stable, where Edgar lived! Edgar was the enormous shire horse who pulled a farm wagon round the gardens and gave everyone rides.

Piggo dashed inside. It *was* Edgar! But what could be *wrong* with him? He was standing in his stable with his great big head lowered down to his great big hairy hooves. "Ooooooh dear me," he said again. "I don't know, I'm sure."

"Edgar!" called Piggo. "Whatever is wrong?"

Edgar looked up, surprised. "Oh, little Piggo," he said. "Hullo."

"What's the *matter*, Edgar?" Piggo asked again.

"It's Clarence," said Edgar, "and Judy."

Clarence was the man who looked after all the animals and Judy helped him when she wasn't at school. She was eleven.

"Clarence and Judy?" Piggo repeated in surprise. "What *about* them?"

"I don't think they like me any more, Piggo," said Edgar. His great big eyes stared mournfully into Piggo's small pink face. "They have taken away my Favourite Thing."

"Not your Favourite Thing!" Piggo whispered. "Not your *Nosebag!*"

Edgar nodded, too heartbroken to speak. "They have given me," he said in the end, "they have given me . . . A PLASTIC BUCKET!"

"Oh no!" gasped Piggo.

Edgar nodded. "A plastic bucket. I don't like that plastic bucket, Piggo. It smells horribly . . . of PLASTIC. It doesn't fit my face, Piggo. It's hard and nasty, not like my nosebag which I've had ever since I was a colt. Oh no, my nosebag is a different matter. It has a soft leather strap behind my ears, the buckle clinks nicely as I chew and I can whiffle my oats about in the bottom. It's *mine*, it fits me and I miss it."

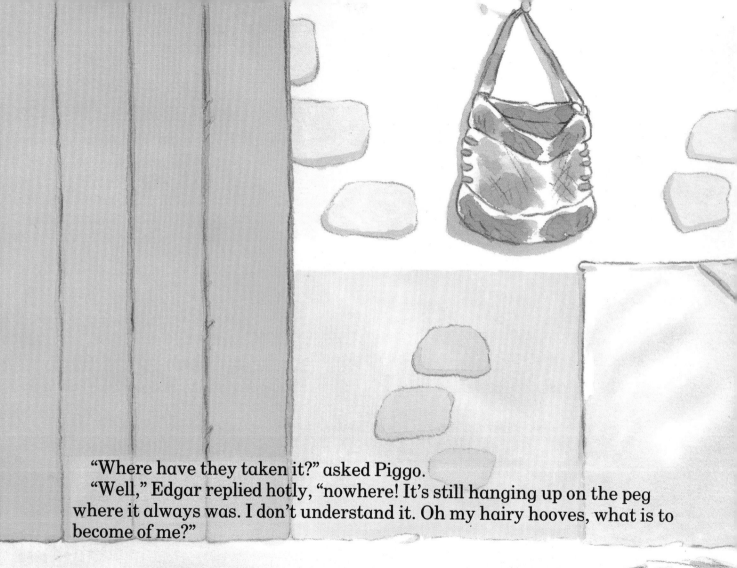

"Where have they taken it?" asked Piggo.

"Well," Edgar replied hotly, "nowhere! It's still hanging up on the peg where it always was. I don't understand it. Oh my hairy hooves, what is to become of me?"

Piggo was desperate to help poor Edgar. He could just see the nosebag hanging on a hook on the stable wall.

"Shall I try to get it down for you, Edgar?" he asked. "Then at least you could see it and sniff it."

"Oh!" sighed Edgar. "For a sniff of my old nosebag – my Favourite Thing. *Could* you, Piggo? Could you really?"

Piggo thought hard. He could reach the nosebag if he stood on the feed bin. But the feed bin was quite tall and made of smooth metal. Then Piggo had one of his stupendous ideas. He would stand on the plastic bucket!

He nudged the horrid bucket until it turned upside down. Then he jumped onto it, put his front feet on top of the feed bin and, with a tremendous spring, brought his back feet up as well.

His trotters slithered on the smooth sloping metal.

"Oh Piggo," exclaimed Edgar, "you've *done* it. Oh you are a brave piglet!"
Piggo was right next to the hanging nosebag. He edged towards it, stood up on his back legs and peered down into the gloomy depths of Edgar's Favourite Thing.

"Can I have it, Piggo?" asked Edgar eagerly, clopping excitedly about in the stable. "Can you get it across to me?"

"No," said Piggo, looking up, "no, I can't."

Edgar was dismayed. "Why not?"

"Because it's full up."

"Full up? FULL UP? What with?"

"It's full up," said Piggo, "with robins."

"Robins?" gasped Edgar.

"Yes," Piggo nodded. "Lots of baby robins in a beautiful warm nest in *your* nosebag, Edgar."

The old horse's face cleared. "Oh I say," he said proudly. "So *that's* why . . . the plastic bucket . . . a robin's nest . . . Well, of course I'm not surprised . . . such a lovely *soft* nosebag after all." Edgar looked radiant with happiness and relief.

They heard voices in the yard outside. It was Clarence and Judy! Piggo was up on the feed bin where he was probably NOT ALLOWED. He stared worriedly across at Edgar.

"In here, Piggo," ordered Edgar, "between my hooves!"

Piggo took a flying leap across the stable, scuttled through the straw and hid in the great hairiness of Edgar's hooves. Only his snout could be seen.

Judy tiptoed in and peeped into the nosebag. "They've got nearly *all* their feathers now! she whispered.

But Clarence had crossed to Edgar and was stroking his long kindly face. "That's good," he said. "Then poor old Edgar can have his nosebag back. I think you've missed it, haven't you boy?" He patted Edgar and they walked out.

When they had gone Edgar carefully parted his enormous white hooves to reveal Piggo in the straw. "Thank you, Piggo," he said and down his soft nostrils he blew a long loving whiffle round the back of Piggo's neck.